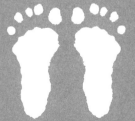

This book belongs to

....

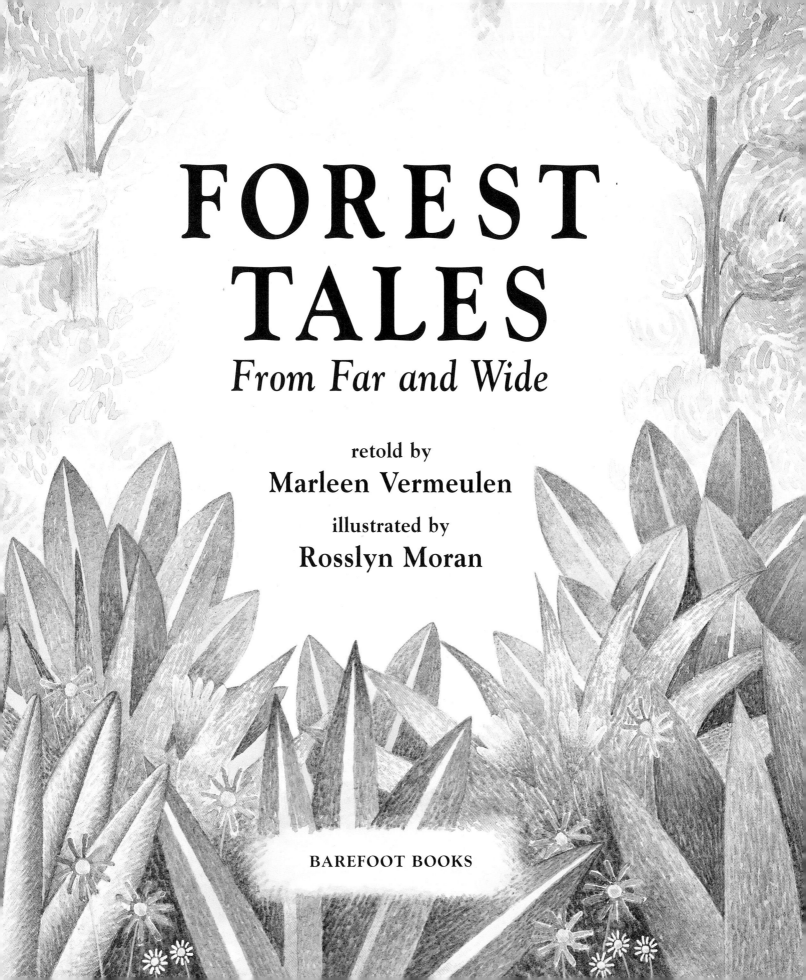

FOREST TALES

From Far and Wide

retold by

Marleen Vermeulen

illustrated by

Rosslyn Moran

BAREFOOT BOOKS

Contents

The Bird and the Mole

Belgian

Once, a young bird was admiring the view she had from her nest high up in an oak tree, in the middle of an ancient forest. "How beautiful it is! I can see the whole world from up here!" she sang boastfully.

Down by the bottom of the tree, in a little hole, lived a small, shy mole. The mole wanted very much to see the view from the bird's nest.

"Bird, Bird, please can I come and see your house?" pleaded the mole.

"Silly mole!" the bird replied, "you can't climb this high. Anyway, it's my house and my house only. Ah! How beautiful it is up here!" she continued.

The mole felt very sad, but he decided to try again. "Bird, Bird, please come and pick me up so that I can see your house! I promise you that if I can see your house, you can come and see mine."

"Nonsense!" laughed the bird. "Your house is nothing but a hole in the ground. I don't want to see that. Go away and stop bothering me!"

So the mole crept back into his house and quietly cried himself to sleep. Meanwhile, the bird settled down comfortably in her nest. Feeling very important she, too, fell asleep.

Then the wind started blowing. The bird woke up with a start. "It's a big storm," she thought and she tried to find somewhere to shelter in her nest. But the wind was blowing stronger and stronger, and soon the rain came pouring down.

"Help!" shouted the bird. "Help me! I'm wet and I'm very cold!"

But no one could hear her and the branches of the tree were swaying wildly from one side to the other.

The bird was now so frightened that she clung frantically to the side of the nest. The wind was blowing stronger and stronger, the rain was pouring harder and harder, and the branches of the tree were swaying wilder and wilder.

"Boohoo, boohoo, boohoo," blew the wind.

"Tick, tick, tick," sang the rain.

"Hush, hush, hush," whispered the trees.

"Help!" cried the bird, "help!" Very slowly she tumbled down through the sky. There was no one who could hear her.

"Boohoo, boohoo, boohoo," blew the wind.

"Tick, tick, tick," sang the rain.

"Hush, hush, hush," whispered the trees.

"BUMP!" Suddenly the bird hit the ground, right in front of the mole's house. She was so frightened and so wet and so cold that she didn't even try to fly up again. Instead, she knocked on the mole's front door. The mole wondered who would want to visit him at a time like this, so when he opened the door, he was very surprised to find the bird in front of him.

"Please let me into your house," begged the bird. "I'm so wet and so cold, and I think I have hurt my wing."

"I didn't think you ever wanted to see my house," responded the mole, "so I think it's better that you leave now."

"Oh, but I need you! Please help me!" sobbed the bird.

"No," said the mole firmly, "you didn't need me before, so it would be silly of me to believe that you need me now. Goodbye, I have many beautiful things to look at in my house."

But just as the mole was about to shuffle back into his hole, the bird shouted, "Stop! I would love to see your house and, if you let me inside now, you can come and see my house as well!"

"All right then," laughed the mole, and proudly he showed the bird around his dark and cozy underground home. For two days he looked after the bird, but her wing was still weak and whenever she tried to fly, "BUMP!" she fell on the ground. Again and again she tried and on the third day, she could finally fly again, up and up and up.

"Look Mole, I can fly again!" cried the bird as she swooped down to him. "Jump on to my back, and I shall take you up to my house."

"Hooray!" cried the mole and he jumped up and down with excitement. Then he climbed carefully on to the bird's back and together they flew up to the bird's house. Now, at last, the mole could see the wonderful view from the bird's nest. From then on, the mole and the bird were the best of friends and they often visited each other.

Bohrah the Kangaroo

Australian

There was once a time when people and animals did not live together. This was the time when kangaroos walked on four legs, not two. This was the time when the nights were darker than dark, with no moon or stars shining in the sky. This was the time when all the animals went out hunting at night. So it was in this dark, dark night that Bohrah the kangaroo went out to look for food.

"Tuf, tuf, tuf, tuf," went Bohrah the kangaroo, as she crept through the forest searching and searching for something to eat.

"Tu-whit, tu-whoo, tu-whit, tu-whoo," called the wise owl.

"Ssss, ssss," hissed the snake.

"Oo-oo-oo, aa-aa-aa," cried the monkey.

One night, while Bohrah the kangaroo was feeding, she saw something and she hid. What was it?

She saw big flames, a fire and people dancing around it.

Bohrah the kangaroo crept closer and closer. But when she was nearly there she took fright, turned around and ran back home.

The next night the same thing happened. Bohrah the kangaroo crept quietly through the forest, hiding behind the trees, when again she saw big flames, a fire and people dancing around it.

As she watched, she started laughing, because it was so funny to see all these people dancing.

Night after night, Bohrah the kangaroo returned to the same place.

"Tuf, tuf, tuf, tuf," she went as she crept through the forest.

"Tu-whit, tu-whoo, tu-whit, tu-whoo, where are you going, Bohrah the kangaroo?" the wise owl wanted to know.

"Ssss, ssss, isss there sssomething I can help you with?" hissed the snake.

"Oo-oo-oo, aa-aa-aa, oo-oo-oo, aa-aa-aa, can I join you?" asked the monkey.

But Bohrah the kangaroo was having a splendid time and she did not want to share her secret with anyone. This continued for a long, long time until one night, while she was hiding behind the trees watching, something strange happened. Her feet started to move and she found that she wanted to dance as well.

"No, no," she thought, "I can't possibly join in. I walk on four legs, the people would notice me straight away."

But as she got up, she tried to stand on two legs and – oops! – she fell down again. She tried and tried again, because she really wanted to dance. But she kept on falling down. This was very disappointing.

"There must be a way. I want to stand on two legs. I want to dance!" she cried. Bohrah the kangaroo was very determined about this.

So she tried one more time, and this time her beautiful tail fell on the ground just between her legs.

There she stood, on two legs, balancing herself with her tail. Then

she jumped into the circle and started dancing along behind the last person in the line. At first the people were shocked and angry. They did not want any animal to disturb their feast.

But as they looked at Bohrah the kangaroo dancing, they started laughing because it was so funny. They all went to look for a false tail of grass, and tied them on to their backs. Then everyone started dancing again, pretending to be kangaroos.

Bohrah the kangaroo went to live with the people and they stayed together as brothers.

Occasionally she visited the other animals. "Tu-whit, tu-whoo, tu-whit, tu-whoo, Ssss, ssss, Oo-oo-oo, aa-aa-aa, oo-oo-oo, aa-aa-aa, Bohrah the kangaroo! Tell us where you live," cried all the animals. They never knew what had happened to her and she never told them.

And ever since that day, kangaroos have always walked on two legs.

Turtle and Monkey Share a Tree

Philippino

One day, a beautiful turtle was sunbathing by the water's edge, when he saw a banana tree floating down the river in his direction.

"I love bananas, and this tree could be mine," he thought. So he jumped into the water, swam to the tree and pulled it up behind him. He pulled and he pulled but, because the tree was big and heavy and the turtle was only small and light, he could not pull the tree out of the water.

"I'll ask the monkey to help me, she's so big and strong," the turtle thought. So he called out, "Monkey, Monkey! Help me, you're so big and strong!"

"Very well," the monkey replied, "but I am not only big and strong, I am also very clever. I will help you drag the tree into the forest, but only if I can have half of the tree!"

The turtle agreed that they

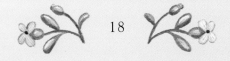

should share the tree, so together they pulled and they pulled, they pulled and they pulled ... and they pulled the tree out of the water and dragged it into the forest.

When they were ready to plant the tree next to the others, the monkey suddenly called, "Stop! This isn't what we agreed. I want my half of the tree now!"

"Don't you think we should plant the tree first and then share the bananas later, once they are fully grown?" the turtle suggested.

"Of course not, you silly turtle," the monkey replied. And looking at the tree, she decided that she wanted the top part which was full of leaves and very beautiful.

So they each took their half of the tree and planted it. Then they waited and waited and waited. The bottom part, which the turtle had planted, had the roots, so it grew into a wonderful, tall banana tree. The top part, which the monkey had planted, had no roots, so it very soon died.

The turtle looked up at his tree and saw lots of fresh, ripe bananas. He tried to climb the tree to pick them. He tried and he tried, but because the tree was big and tall and the turtle was only small and light, he kept falling down.

"I'll ask the monkey to help me, she's so big and strong," the turtle said to himself.

"Monkey, Monkey! Please help me, please climb the tree and throw down all the ripe bananas! Monkey, Monkey! Help me,

you're so big and strong," the turtle begged the monkey.

But the monkey was cross because her half of the tree had not grown any bananas. She thought that the turtle had given her the bad part of the tree. So the monkey climbed the tree and ate all the bananas herself, throwing down nothing but the skins.

"Give me some bananas!" the turtle screamed. "Give me some bananas! They belong to me!"

But the monkey did not take the slightest bit of notice. So while she was eating the bananas the turtle decided to play a trick on her. He gathered lots of spiky branches and thorns and placed them by the foot of the tree. Then he hid, and waited and waited and waited.

After she had finished eating the last banana, the monkey leapt down, landing right on top of the thorns. "Ouch! Ouch! Just you wait until I catch you!" she cried, jumping up and down in pain. "Ouch! This really hurts! Turtle, where are you? Come out and show yourself!"

Now the turtle was really much cleverer than the monkey and he had been expecting this. He crept out meekly from behind the bush and whispered, "Monkey, you can do anything you like, but please don't throw me in the water."

"You silly turtle," laughed the monkey, "that is exactly what I am going to do!" And she hurled the turtle into the water. Then she brushed her hands together, feeling very pleased with herself. But from the safety of the river, the turtle poked his head out and called, "Thank you, thank you, Monkey! For don't you know that we turtles love the water best! Thank you very much!"

Then the turtle swam happily away, and he took care never to ask a monkey for help again.

Goldilocks and the Three Bears

English

Once upon a time there was a very big bear, a middle-sized bear and a tiny little bear. They lived in a beautiful cottage in the middle of a forest.

One morning just before breakfast the very big bear, who had a very big voice, said to the others, "Let's go out for a walk in the forest."

The middle-sized bear answered in her middle-sized voice, "What a good idea! That will allow our porridge to cool down."

The tiny little bear piped up in his tiny little voice, "Let's go now while it's still early!"

So off they went into the forest. The very big bear went first, walking with very big steps, then the middle-sized bear, walking with middle-sized steps, and last came the tiny little bear, walking with tiny little steps.

Now while the three bears were in the woods, a girl named Goldilocks was walking nearby when she smelled the delicious porridge. The door of the cottage was open, and so she went in. There she saw a table, with three bowls of porridge on it. Goldilocks looked around, and did not see anyone. So she decided to eat the porridge. First, she lifted a very big spoon and tasted the very big bear's porridge, but that was too hot.

Then, with a middle-sized spoon, she tasted the middle-sized bear's porridge, but that was too cold. Finally, taking a tiny little spoon, she tasted the tiny little bear's porridge. That was perfect, so she ate it all up.

Feeling tired after eating this tasty porridge, Goldilocks decided to sit down. She looked around the room, and saw three chairs. First she sat in the very big chair, but it was much too hard. Then Goldilocks tried the middle-sized chair, but that was much too soft. Finally she tried the tiny little chair. That was perfect, but – CRACK! – the chair broke and she fell on her bottom onto the floor.

Goldilocks was very cross. She still felt tired, so she went upstairs to look for somewhere to rest. There she found a bedroom. She looked around the room, and saw three beds. First she climbed onto the very big bed, but that was too high. Then she climbed onto the middle-sized bed, but that was too low. Finally, she tried the tiny little bed, and that was perfect. She lay down and fell asleep.

Soon the three bears came home, looking forward to eating their porridge. But when they sat down, the very big bear exclaimed in his very big voice, "Someone has tried to eat my porridge!"

Then the middle-sized bear said in her middle-sized voice, "Someone has tried to eat my porridge, too!"

Finally, the tiny little bear cried in his tiny little voice, "Someone has tried to eat my porridge and has finished it all up!"

After this, the bears looked around the room. Goldilocks had not put the cushions back in their places on the chairs, and the very big bear said in his very big voice, "Someone has been sitting in my chair!"

Then the middle-sized bear spoke in her middle-sized voice, "Someone has been sitting in my chair, too!"

Finally, the tiny little bear whispered in his tiny little voice, "Someone has been sitting in my chair – and has broken it all to pieces!"

The three bears were very angry. Next, they went up to the bedroom, where Goldilocks had left their beds in a big mess. The very big bear growled in his very big voice, "Someone has been sleeping in my bed!"

Then the middle-sized bear sighed in her middle-sized voice, "Someone has been sleeping in my bed, too!"

Finally, the tiny little bear sobbed in his tiny little voice, "Someone has been sleeping in my bed – and she's still there!"

At this, Goldilocks woke up with a start. When she saw the three bears, she was very frightened and ran straight out of the house and back through the forest. The three bears have never seen her since.

The Little Elephant

Indian

In the deepest depths of a forest in India, there lived a baby elephant with his family. As you probably know, in India it gets very, very hot, so most animals do special things to cool themselves down. Now this baby elephant had a real problem – he didn't know how to cool down.

One hot day, the baby elephant went for a walk by himself. As he walked, he got hotter and hotter, until he was so hot he could bear it no longer. The baby elephant called to a bird who was flying nearby.

"Bird, Bird, please can you tell me how to cool down?"

"Caw, caw," answered the bird. "It's easy. You just fly from branch to branch and the breeze keeps you cool." With that, the bird flew off.

The baby elephant looked at his front legs and he looked at his back legs. He tried to flap them like

wings, but he did not go up in the sky. "I will never be able to fly high like the bird," he thought sadly, "and this doesn't cool me down at all!"

The baby elephant continued on his journey, feeling even hotter than before. After a while he met a snake.

"Snake, Snake, please can you tell me how to cool down?" asked the baby elephant.

"Ssss, ssss," whispered the snake, "That's easssy. You jussst curl your

body around the trunk of a tree and you ssstay nice and cool." With that the snake curled up around the tree and dozed off.

The baby elephant looked at his front legs and he looked at his back legs. He flung them around the trunk, so that it looked as if he was hugging the tree. But it felt very uncomfortable and soon he fell – BAM! – onto the ground. Feeling sad and sore, he picked himself up again, thinking, "I will never be able to curl my body around the tree like the snake, and this doesn't cool me down at all!"

The baby elephant walked farther into the forest, feeling very hot and tired. Suddenly he saw a tiger!

"Tiger, Tiger, please can you tell me how to cool down?" pleaded the baby elephant.

"Mmmm, mmmm," replied the tiger, licking his lips. "It's nearly lunch-time," he thought, so he said, "Just come a little closer to me and I'll tell you." The tiger felt like eating the baby elephant for lunch, so he called to him again. "Come right beside me, or you won't hear what I have to say."

The baby elephant understood what the tiger was trying to do and so he ran away as fast as he could. Luckily the tiger was feeling too hot to run after him.

At last the baby elephant stopped running, and fell down in the grass. He was so very hot that he started to cry.

A crocodile happened to be passing by. "It's a nice hot day, why are you crying?" asked the crocodile.

"It's no use, I want to cool down and no one can tell me how!" sobbed the baby elephant.

"Snap, snap," laughed the crocodile. "That's easy. Just follow me and we'll have you nice and cool in a jiffy!"

The baby elephant slowly got to his feet and followed the crocodile, who took him to a river that wound through the forest. The crocodile jumped into the river and started splashing about. "Come on, Elephant, come in and join me!"

At first the baby elephant thought, "I will never be able to splash about like the crocodile." But then he put one foot in the river, and another, and another, and another. "Ah!" he thought. "This feels good."

He smiled at the crocodile and together they splashed and played in the river. "This is fun!" he shouted.

And from that day on, whenever the baby elephant was hot, he just went to the river and played with his friend the crocodile. "This is fun!" he would shout, spraying the water through his trunk and flapping his great big ears.

The Baboons and the Bees

Kenyan

In a thick forest in Kenya lived a family of baboons. They loved eating the leaves, berries and nuts that grew wild in the forest. They were very happy living like this until, one year, it stopped raining. The land got drier and drier, and the animals got hotter and hotter because there was no water; the trees and plants couldn't grow any more. There were no more leaves, berries or nuts to eat. Soon the baboons were miserable and very, very hungry.

Chief Baboon knew he had to find a way to save his family. He crawled through the forest, crept over branches, pushed his way through the bushes, when suddenly he heard a buzzing noise. He looked up and saw a swarm of bees. They looked fat and well-fed.

"Food!" thought the baboon. "The honey from these bees could feed my whole family!"

Because he couldn't carry the honey alone, he decided to get his family to help him. So the next morning they all set off together, hoping to find enough honey to feed everyone.

As soon as the bees left their hive in the trees, the baboons climbed up the branches, collected all the honey they could find, then quickly ran home.

Now bees always leave the smallest bee behind to guard the hive, and when the bees got back that evening they scolded the little one for letting their honey go.

"Some men with faces like dogs came and stole the honey. I couldn't do anything," cried the little bee.

"Go and find them! Show us where they are!" shouted the bees.

"Please come with me, help me, I can't do this alone," sobbed the little bee.

So they all flew off together, the little bee in the middle, protected by the others, trying to find the animals who had stolen their honey. They came to a herd of buffaloes.

"Are these the animals who stole the honey?" asked the queen bee.

"No," replied the little bee, "these are not the animals who came to the hive."

They flew on and saw some lions.

"Are these the animals who stole the honey?" asked the queen bee.

"No," replied the little bee, "these are not the animals who came to the hive."

They flew on and saw some antelopes.

"Are these the animals who stole the honey?" asked the queen bee.

. But again the little bee replied, "No, these are not the animals who came to the hive."

They saw tigers, snakes, giraffes and many more animals. Finally, they came upon the family of baboons.

The baboons were happy. They were feasting on the delicious honey because they knew they had enough to feed them for the rest of the month.

Suddenly, the swarm of bees arrived and set upon the baboons, stinging them everywhere. They stung their noses and cheeks, their bellies and ears, their chins and heads. The baboons tried to run away through the forest, hide under the rocks or climb to the top of the highest trees, but the bees followed them everywhere.

At last the baboons dove under the water where the bees couldn't reach them.

"We are much smaller than you, but we can punish you for stealing our honey!" said the queen bee.

"We will give you back your honey, if you stop stinging us!" responded the chief baboon. The queen bee agreed to this.

So the baboons showed the bees where they had stored their honey.

"We're very sorry we stole your food," said the chief baboon, "but we were starving and I didn't have any food to feed my children."

"We know of a forest where there is plenty of food," replied the queen bee. "If you go there you will be able to feed everyone in your family."

The baboons set off and traveled for days. When they reached the forest, full of trees covered with dark green leaves, they knew they could live there happily forever. They also knew that they would never steal honey again.

The Wolf and the Seven Kids

German

Once a mother goat lived with her seven kids at the edge of the forest. On the other side of the forest lived a big wolf, who everybody feared.

"I am the best, I am the strongest!" he always bragged.

Sometimes, Mother Goat had to go into the forest to find food for her kids. Just before leaving she always told them to be careful of the wolf.

So Mother Goat set off one morning and on her way she bumped into the wolf. "Oh, Wolf," she said, "please can we be friends?"

"Stupid goat," the wolf replied, "don't you realize that I am the big wolf, the king of the forest? How could I be friends with a goat?"

Sadly, Mother Goat continued on her way while the wolf ran off through the forest, laughing and laughing.

The wolf started to feel a bit tired

after all that running, and when he realized that he was near the goats' house, he decided to ask the little goats if he could rest there.

"Please, dear little kids, may I come into your house?" he called.

But the clever kids knew that they could not trust the wolf, so they said, "Go away, you terrible wolf, go and find somewhere else to rest."

The wolf did not like this reply. "Mmm," he thought, "I will play a trick on them. I need to do something that makes me seem less like a wolf."

"Tu-whit, tu-whoo!" He pretended to be an owl, but that was too difficult.

"Miaow, miaow!" He tried to sound like a cat, but his voice was too deep.

"Squeak, squeak!" But he was too big to be a mouse.

What could he do so that the little goats would let him in?

He sat outside the goats' house wondering what to do when

suddenly he saw a pot of white paint. The wolf remembered that goats have white feet, so he carefully covered his feet one by one with the white paint. He then knocked on the door, showing only his white feet.

"Who's there?" the little goats asked.

"It is your mother," the wolf replied, trying to make his voice sound as soft as possible. This time the kids believed him. So they

opened the door and let him in.

The wolf suddenly felt hungry, so he said, "Now I will eat you all up!"

"No, Wolf!" screamed the little goats, "first let us play a game."

"Well, I'm hungry – but what is the game about?" the wolf asked.

"It is called hide-and-seek. You close your eyes and we hide. Then you look for us, and when you find us, you can eat us," laughed the kids.

"Oh, very well," growled the wolf. "This will be easy! I will find you in no time!'

As soon as he closed his eyes the little goats hid themselves in all the best possible places. The wolf searched and searched but he could not find them. After a while he felt so worn out that he lay down to sleep. He was still snoring when Mother Goat got home. As soon as she saw the wolf there, she quickly tied him up. Then she called to her clever kids and they all jumped out of their hiding places. "What do you think, children, shall we roast or fry the wolf?" she asked.

"Roast him. No, fry him. Roast! Fry!" argued the kids.

They made such a noise that the wolf woke up. "Please, Mother Goat," he begged, "please don't eat me! I promise I'll be good and I'll look after your kids whenever you want me to!"

So that is what happened. The goats carefully untied the wolf and set him free. After this, he came to visit the goat family as often as he could. The wolf became quite a different character and the kids always asked to play hide-and-seek with him!

Sources for the Stories

The Bird and the Mole
Because I specialize in stories that have strong dramatic possibilities, I sometimes write my own stories, which children can act out. This is one of them.

Bohrah the Kangaroo
This story was first recorded by Catherine Langloh Parker, who grew up among the Aborigines of Australia. It was published as "The Kangaroo Dance" in *Australian Legendary Tales* (London, 1896), the first anthology of Aboriginal tales to be published in English.

Turtle and Monkey Share a Tree
This story is taken from *Ride with the Sun — An Anthology of Folk Tales and Stories from the United Nations* edited by Harold Courlander, (Whittesley House, New York, 1955).

Goldilocks and the Three Bears
This popular nursery story was first published in 1837 in a collection by Robert Southey, *The Little Doctor*. In Southey's version, the intruder is a little old woman; later she developed into Silverhair, and finally into the young girl, Goldilocks.

The Little Elephant
This story was given to me by Shanti Brahmachari, who learned it during her childhood in India. I met Shanti in 1990. As the Youth and Education Director at the Tricycle Theater in Kilburn, London, she employed me to run drama workshops for children under five and this is one of many stories and anecdotes she shared with me.

The Baboons and the Bees
This story is taken from *Beautiful Nyakio*, by Frederick Ndung'u (East African Publishing House, Nairobi, Kenya, 1968).

The Wolf and the Seven Kids
This is my variation of the Grimm Brothers' story, first published in their *Kinder- und Hausmärchen* (1812).

Barefoot Beginners — an imprint of Barefoot Book Ltd, PO Box 95, Kingswood, Bristol BS30 5BH, United Kingdom.   Text copyright © 1998 by Marleen Vermeulen. Illustrations copyright © 1998 by Rosslyn Moran. The moral right of Marleen Vermeulen and Rosslyn Moran to be identified as the author and illustrator of this work has been asserted. ISBN: 1 901223 33 7
  Graphic design by Judy Linard. Color separation by Scanner Services, Verona.
Printed and bound in Singapore by Tien Wah Press Pte Ltd

BAREFOOT BOOKS publishes high-quality picture books for
children of all ages and specializes in the work of artists and writers from
many cultures. If you have enjoyed this book and would like to receive a copy of
our current catalogue, please contact our London office – tel: 011 44 171 704 6492
fax: 011 44 171 359 5798 email: sales@barefoot-books.com
website: www.barefoot-books.com